Say Please to the Honeybees

Story by: Susan Ross

Art by: Megan Stive

This book belongs to:

_____

Books written by Susan Ross and Illustrated by Megan Stiver

The Great Bellybutton Cover-up
The Kit Kat Caper
Say Please to the Honeybees
The Rose and the Lily

No part of this publication may be reproduced in whole or in part, or transmitted by any form or by any means without the written permission of the author.
For information regarding permission please e-mail Susan Ross at susanhermanross@yahoo.ca.

Copyright © 2010 by Susan Ross
All rights reserved.

Library and Archives Canada Cataloguing in Publication

Ross, Susan, 1954-
   Say please to the honeybees / story by Susan
Ross ; art by Megan Stiver.

ISBN 978-0-9810634-3-0

1. Sheep--Juvenile fiction. I. Stiver, Megan, 1988- II. Title.

PS8635.O698S29 2010   jC813'.6   C2010-901073-6

Layout by Megan Stiver.
Production in Canada by Images, London, Ontario (www.images.ca)

Susan (Herman) Ross is a former teacher who lives in London, Ontario with her husband, Nathan, and a house full of animals.

Megan Stiver is currently studying illustration at Sheridan College in Oakville, Ontario.

A Special Thank You

To all the children and school librarians in London, Ontario and friends and family who contributed to my book with their suggestions, comments and feedback. You motivated me to change my story until it was just right. Thank you, as well, to Susan Dean for her editing expertise and Megan for bringing Violet to life.

About the Book

Susan created the original story, **The Great Bellybutton Cover-up**, for a sheep shearing event at Fanshawe Pioneer Village in London, Ontario. The illustrations are modelled after Fanshawe Pioneer Village, although artistic license has been used. The real Violet was sheared at this event. **Say Please to the Honeybees** is the second 'Violet' story.

Dedication

Say Please to the Honeybees is dedicated, in loving memory, to Healey Illouz, Tali Cohen and Bill Bot.

It was Violet's first visit to Pioneer Village. The fluffy, white sheep noticed a beehive hanging from a short branch on a tall tree. Honey was trickling down its sides.

"Hmmmmm, I've heard that honey is delicious," thought Violet.

Did Violet politely ask the bees, "May I have some honey, please?" No, she did not.

Instead, that sneaky sheep tiptoed over to the beehive. She swiped her hoof in the honey and tasted it.

"Mmmmmm, honey is yummy,"
Violet mumbled while smacking her lips.
She began gobbling up the sweet treat.

Violet was a very messy eater.
She was dribbling honey all over
her soft, fluffy, white wool.

Queen Beeatrice witnessed the robbery and roared, "There's a sheep stealing our honey! Get that honey back!"

The honeybees swarmed out of their hive. They tried to get the honey off Violet, but got stuck in the sticky stuff instead.

Six-year-old Molly saw poor Violet and shouted, "Help, that poor sheep is covered in bees!"

Violet's owner, Farmer Shepherd, heard the call for help. He rushed over with a smoker and smoked the bees off Violet.

The angry honeybees headed back towards their hive, vowing revenge.

Violet's wool was now a dirty, sticky, gooey mess! She needed to be sheared.

Farmer Shepherd led Violet over to the village's sheep shearing contest. Violet was so upset by her disgraceful appearance that she didn't move a muscle when Farmer Shepherd cut off all her flawed fleece. He was finished in the blink of an eye and won the fifty dollar prize.

Embarrassed by her bareness, Violet decided to hide in a haystack in the barn. Weary from her hair-raising morning, Violet was soon napping, snuggled under the hay.

Something tiny tickled Violet's nose.

Spiders were sitting on Violet's snout! They had spied the delicious honey that had soaked through Violet's wool.

Did the spiders politely ask Violet, "May we have some honey, please?" No, they did not.

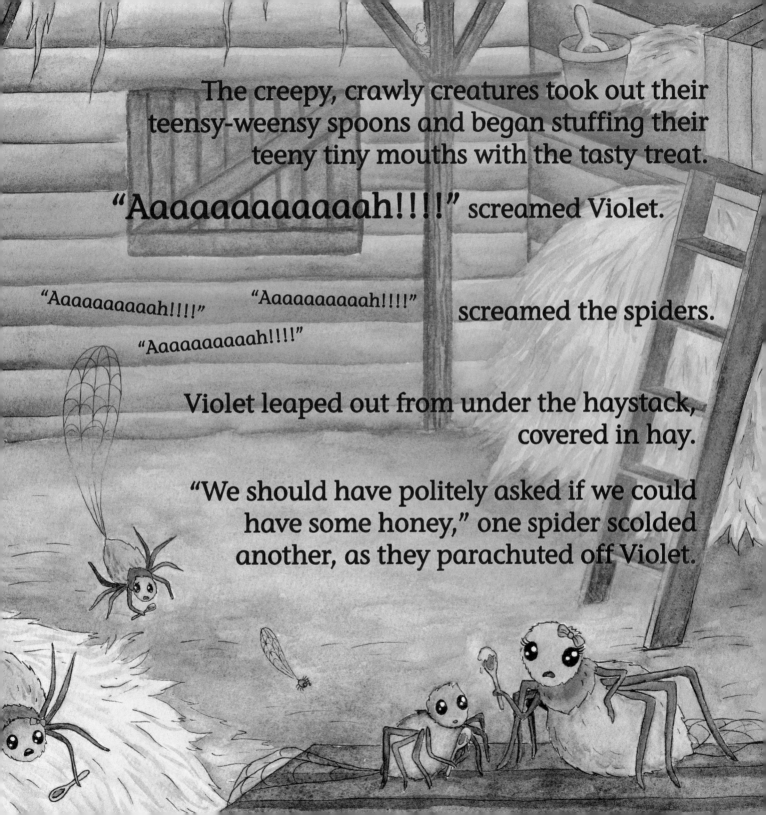

The creepy, crawly creatures took out their teensy-weensy spoons and began stuffing their teeny tiny mouths with the tasty treat.

"Aaaaaaaaaaaaah!!!!" screamed Violet.

"Aaaaaaaaaaah!!!!"   "Aaaaaaaaaaah!!!!"   screamed the spiders.

"Aaaaaaaaaaah!!!!"

Violet leaped out from under the haystack, covered in hay.

"We should have politely asked if we could have some honey," one spider scolded another, as they parachuted off Violet.

The village's huge horse, Harry, was horribly hungry. He discovered Violet in the middle of his corral, swatting at the few remaining spiders.

Did Harry politely ask Violet, "May I have some hay, please?" No, he did not.

Harry just trotted over to Violet and began munching on the honey-sweetened hay.

"Stop it!" Violet demanded. "You're slobbering all over me, you greedy pig!"

"Oink, oink," said Harry the horse, and he continued chomping on the hay until it was all gone.

Embarrassed by her bareness, Violet dashed towards the schoolhouse to hide. She tripped over the school bell's rope and somersaulted in the garden. Flowers stuck to her sticky body.

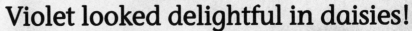
Violet looked delightful in daisies!

Violet was enjoying the visitors' compliments when she heard a deafening "Bzzzzz." She knew it wasn't the sound of shears; all the shearing was finished.

Uh oh! A huge swarm of bees was coming straight for Violet and her daisies. Everyone dashed for cover; everyone except Violet, who was frozen in fear.

Did the honeybees politely ask Violet, "May we have some daisies, please?" No, they definitely did not.

Each bee grabbed a daisy. Then they all flew away snickering.

Queen Beeatrice bellowed, "Next time leave our honey alone, you shifty sheep!"

"I didn't like those droopy daisies anyway!" Violet hollered back, shaking her fist. She wiped a tear from her eye and whispered, "Yes, I did."

Violet was now dirty and sticky and hot.
"I need a bath," she thought.

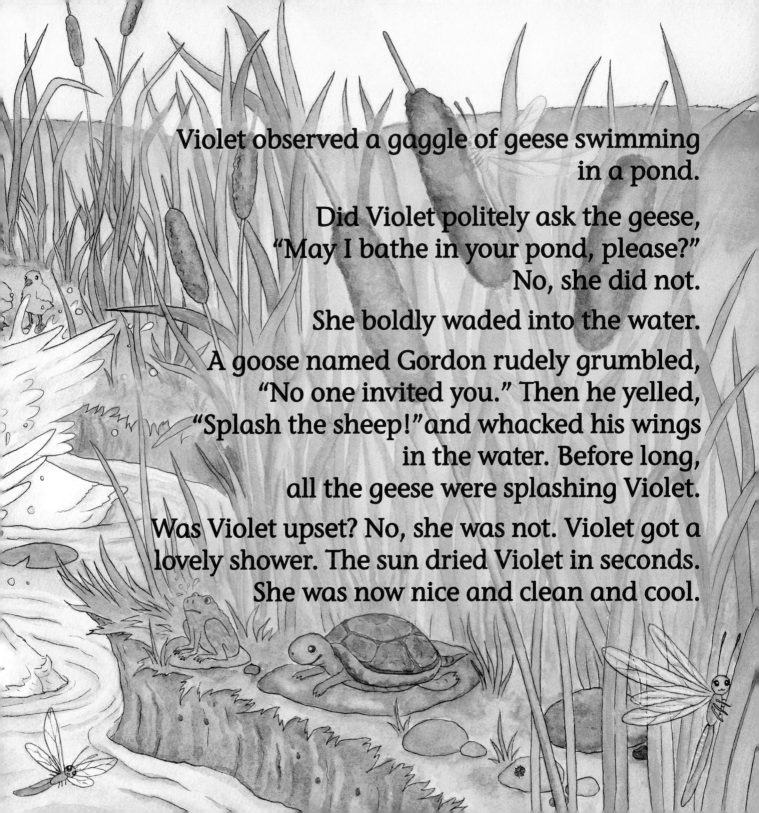

Violet observed a gaggle of geese swimming in a pond.

Did Violet politely ask the geese, "May I bathe in your pond, please?" No, she did not.

She boldly waded into the water.

A goose named Gordon rudely grumbled, "No one invited you." Then he yelled, "Splash the sheep!" and whacked his wings in the water. Before long, all the geese were splashing Violet.

Was Violet upset? No, she was not. Violet got a lovely shower. The sun dried Violet in seconds. She was now nice and clean and cool.

Embarrassed by her bareness, Violet was looking for a place to hide. She slinked past the church, the blacksmith and the print shop. When she got to the general store, however, Violet came to a sudden stop. There, in the window, was a vivid violet sweater. It was decorated with a picture of a fluffy Violet!

Did Violet politely ask the shopkeeper, "May I have the sweater, please?" No, she did not.

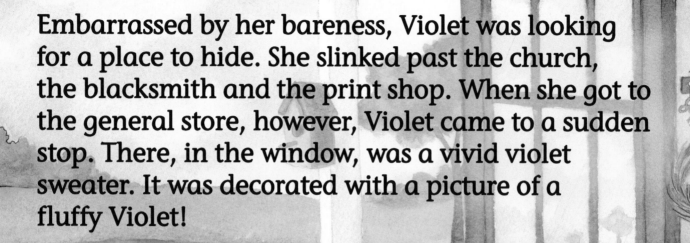

Violet simply whisked the sweater out of the window and wiggled and wriggled until it covered her perfectly.

"Take that sweater off!" ordered the shocked shopkeeper.
Violet merely motioned that the sweater had her picture on it.

Molly had just bought a peppermint candy stick. She rushed out of the store and found Farmer Shepherd. She told him about the sheep, the sweater and the salesperson.

Farmer Shepherd hurried back to the general store. Violet looked at him with puppy dog eyes. "Pleeeease," she said.

What was Farmer Shepherd to do?

He took out his wallet, removed the prize money, and handed it to the shopkeeper. He didn't want Violet to be embarrassed by her bareness anymore.

"This sweater now belongs to Violet. She looks vibrant in vivid violet!" Farmer Shepherd declared.

Violet gave Farmer Shepherd a big hug.

When Violet returned home, she immediately strutted to the barn to show off her new look to all her furry and feathered friends. The animals thought Violet looked spectacular in her violet sweater.

The sheep, the pigs, the cows and the chickens all went to Farmer Shepherd's farmhouse. They all politely asked, "May we have sweaters too, pleeeease?"

That winter, visitors to the Shepherd farm were surprised to see every single animal wearing its own stylish sweater!

Honeybees

Bees are very fuzzy,
Circled with black rings.
They have two antennae
And two sets of wings.

They also have a stinger.
It's sharp as it can be.
They have six legs to crawl with.
I hope they stay off me.

I wonder if you know that
Bees really have five eyes.
We see only two though;
I bet they'd make great spies.

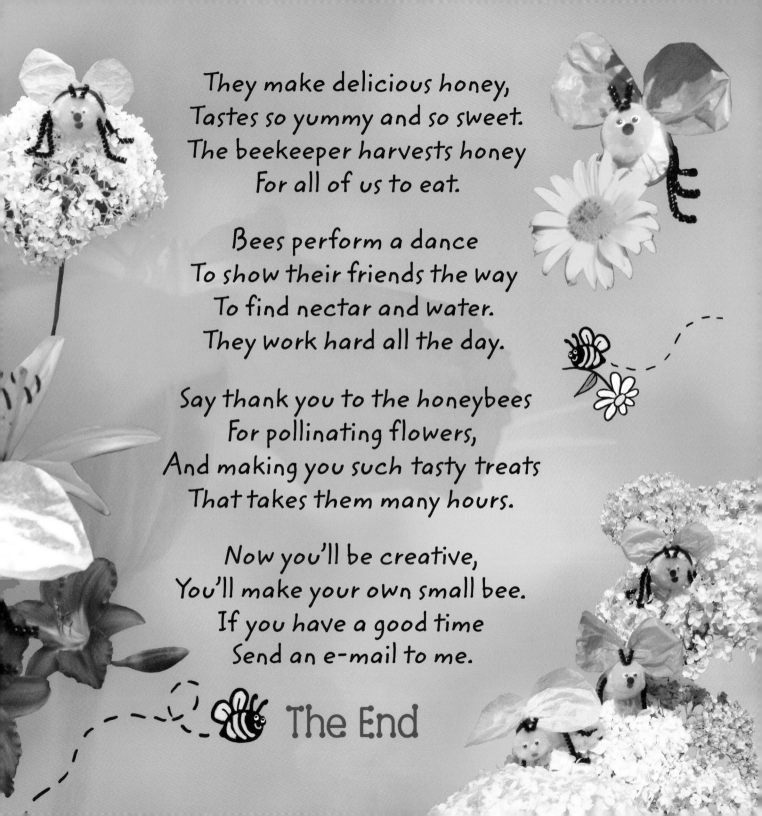

They make delicious honey,
Tastes so yummy and so sweet.
The beekeeper harvests honey
For all of us to eat.

Bees perform a dance
To show their friends the way
To find nectar and water.
They work hard all the day.

Say thank you to the honeybees
For pollinating flowers,
And making you such tasty treats
That takes them many hours.

Now you'll be creative,
You'll make your own small bee.
If you have a good time
Send an e-mail to me.

The End

Be A Busy Bee, Make a Busy Bee

Supplies:

- 1" Styrofoam ball
- two 12" pipecleaners
- 1" yellow pompom
- construction paper
- white glue
- yellow tissue paper (a different colour can be used for the wings)
- scissors
- googly eyes (optional)
- 5 mm pompom (optional)
- toothpick

Instructions:

1. Wrap the Styrofoam ball in a 5" (12.5 cm) square of yellow tissue paper and secure the ends with glue.

2.  Glue the yellow pompom onto the Styrofoam ball where you secured the tissue paper.

3. Cut 1 pipecleaner into six equal pieces (2"/5cm). This will make 6 legs.

- Bend the 6 pieces into 'legs' as shown in the picture.
- Make three tiny holes with a toothpick on each side of the Styrofoam ball, then insert the leg

4.   Cut two or three 2" x ¼" (5cm x 5mm) pieces of black construction paper and glue them onto the ball for the bee's stripes.

5.  Cut two 1" (3 cm) pieces from the second pipecleaner. Make a tiny hole with a toothpick in the back end of the bee and insert one piece as a stinger.

6. Cut a piece of tissue paper 4" x 2½" (10cm x 6cm).

- Twist it in half to form wings.
- Round off the corners with scissors.
- Glue it to the bee's back.

7.  Fold the second piece of 1" (2.5cm) pipecleaner into a 'V'. Glue it onto the top of the pompom head as the bee's antennae.

8. Place the facial features on the face. Use circles cut from construction paper for the eyes and nose. Cut a circle in half for the mouth. Use a hole puncher if you have one. (Googly eyes can be used for eyes. A tiny pompom can be used for the nose.)

Make your own creation!
Use your imagination!

CPSIA information can be obtained
at www.ICGtesting.com
Printed in the USA
LVIC06n2305041216
515802LV00012B/31

Make Your Own Bee!

Say Please to the Honeybees

Say Please to the Honeybees continues the adventures of Violet, the sheep. Taking honey from the bees without saying "please" lands Violet in a heap of trouble. Violet is plagued by bees seeking comical revenge, spiders wanting tasty treats, a hungry horse, a gaggle of geese and a snippy shopkeeper. Children will love this humorous story with its adorable ending. Read The Great Bellybutton Cover-up for more of Violet's hilarious antics.

ISBN 978-0-9810634-3-0
50995

9 780981 063430

Craft Instructions Inclu

T3-BMG-424